It's beginning
to look a lot like
Rex-mas.

written by Amy Fellner Dominy
& Nate Evans

illustrated by AG Ford

SCHOLASTIC INC.

ISBN 978-1-338-62554-7

12 11 10 9 8 7 6 5 4 3 2 1 19 20 21 22 23 24

Printed in the U.S.A. 40

First Scholastic printing, November 2019

This book is set in Billy/Fontspring; GillSans/Monotype.
Designed by Beth Meyers

For the librarians who encouraged our love of reading,
and the teachers who inspired us to write.

—A.F.D. and N.E.

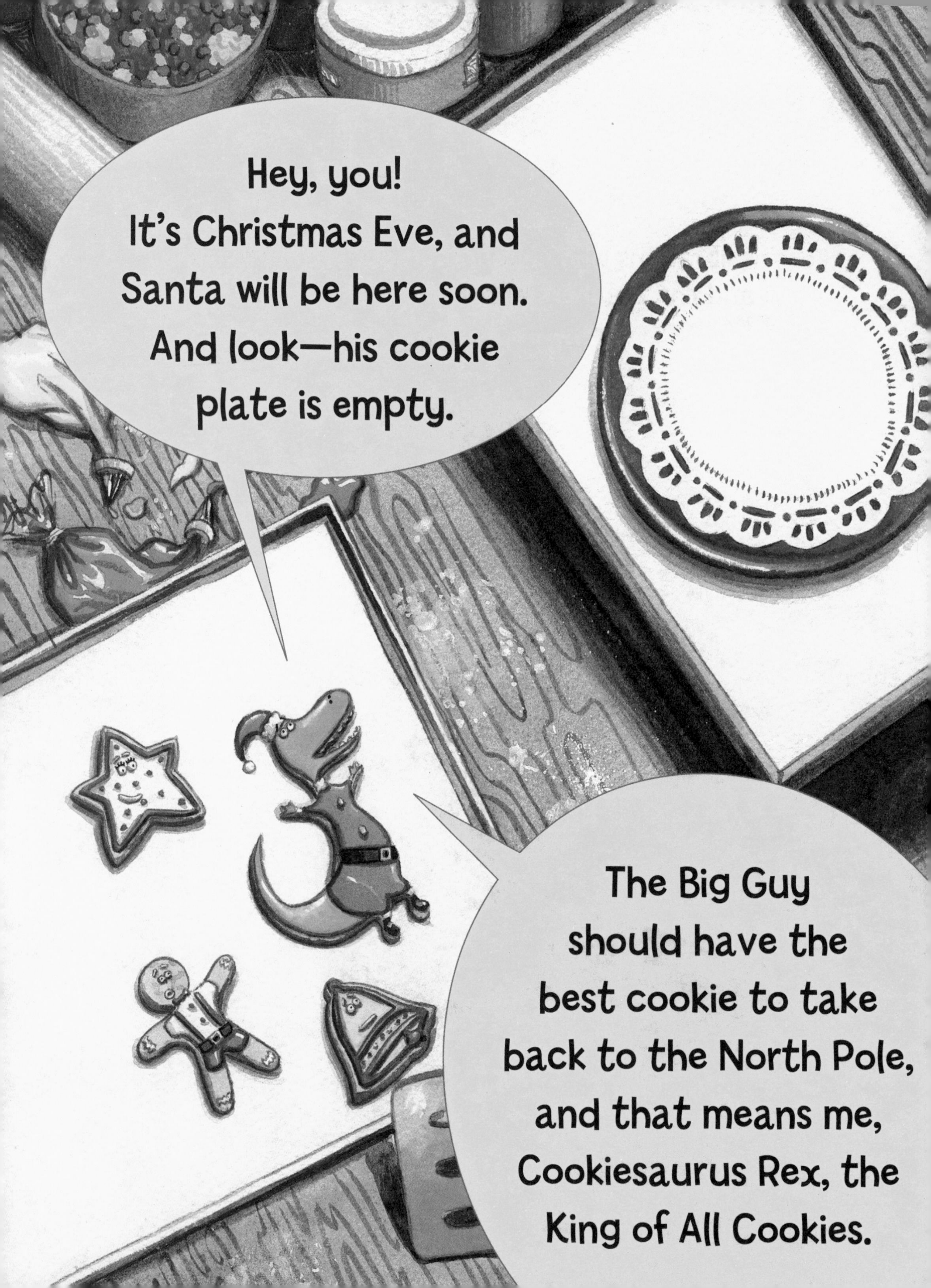
Hey, you!
It's Christmas Eve, and
Santa will be here soon.
And look—his cookie
plate is empty.
The Big Guy
should have the
best cookie to take
back to the North Pole,
and that means me,
Cookiesaurus Rex, the
King of All Cookies.

But does anyone think of dinosaurs at Christmas?
Is there a dinosaur on every Christmas tree? Are dinos hung by the chimney with care?
No! And it's not fair. Dinos have Christmas spirit too!

Me! Pick me!
Come on,
Mr. Spatula.

See what I mean?
What's so special about Star?
Is it because she twinkles?
Because I can tinkle too . . .
I mean TWINKLE!

Where are you going? Santa doesn't need a glass of milk. He needs another cookie. Like me!

If only I
could fly . . .
Wait! I can!

Oops.

Where did Star go? Uhhhh . . . maybe she was a shooting star? Good thing *I'm* here to save the day. Now you can give Santa a real present—ME!

No!
Don't put me back!
I want to be Santa's
cookie.

Bell gets to be the
lucky one?
You're picking that
ding-dong?

I’m coming over, Bell!

Yahooooo!

Double oops.

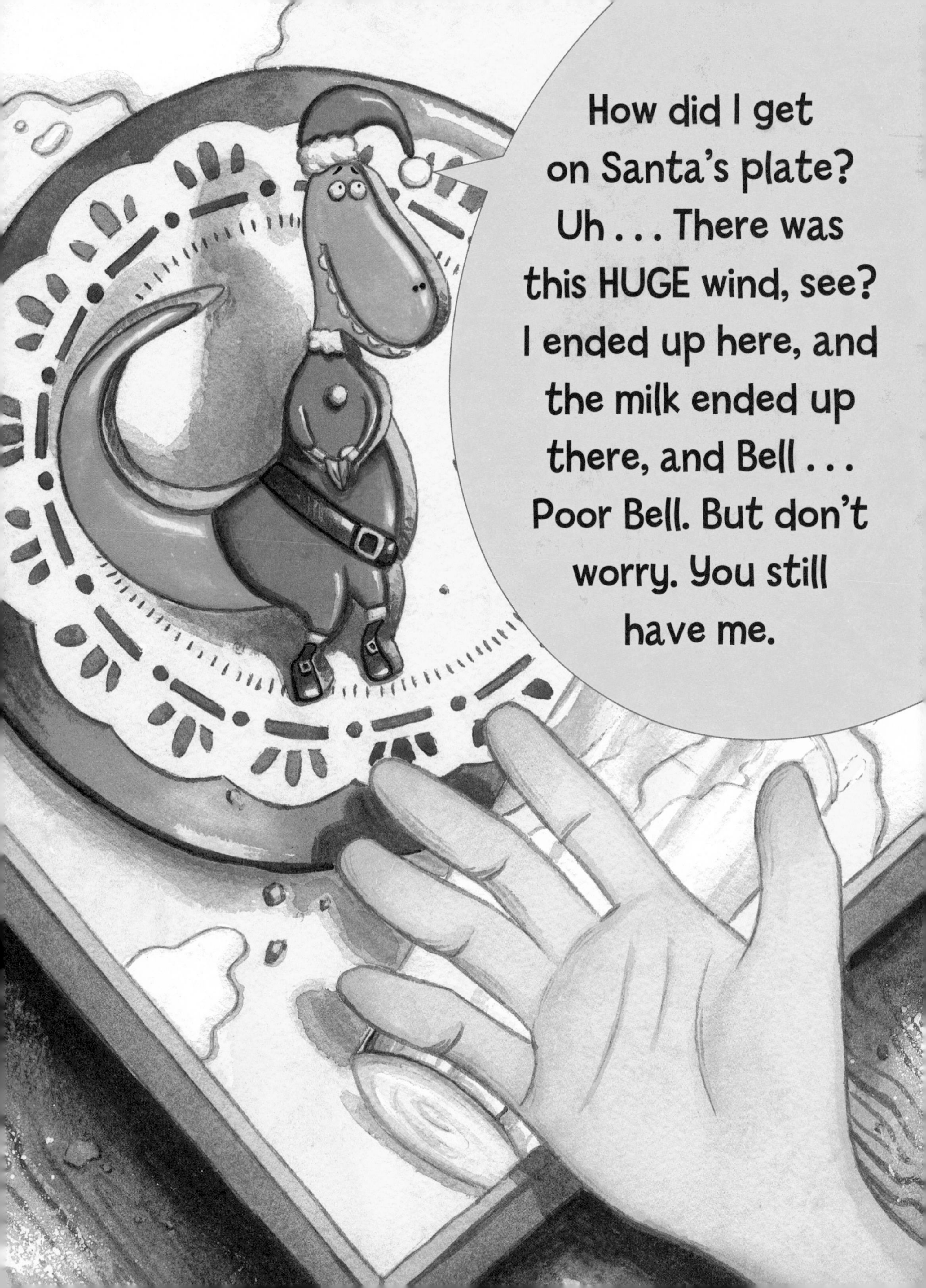
How did I get on Santa's plate? Uh . . . There was this HUGE wind, see? I ended up here, and the milk ended up there, and Bell . . . Poor Bell. But don't worry. You still have me.

Where are you going with me? You can't leave Santa's plate empty!

Wait one stinkin', stompin' minute!

Why can't it be me? I'm green, aren't I? And look, I have a mistle-*toe*. *I* should be Santa's cookie and get to ride on his sleigh and play reindeer games.

I'm making my move.
It's go time!

Catch me,
Gingerbread Boy!

Triple oops.

For Santa
There you are! I don't know what happened to Ginger. But look at Santa's plate. It's still empty, and he'll be here any minute!

Hello, Mr. Spatula.
Wheeeee, I'm flying!
It's really for real this time! I'm going to be Santa's cookie. North Pole, here I come!
Santa

For Santa
How do I look, guys?
Guys? Buddies?
Oh no. What have
I done?

I'm a *crummy* cookie! Santa's going to put me at the top of his *Naughty List.* I only wanted to show that I had Christmas spirit too. I didn't mean to hurt anyone. It just sort of happened.

FoR
Santa

FoR
Santa

This is where you guys belong.
FoR
Santa

Don't worry about me.
I'll just be over here ALL alone.
No one wants a dinosaur
for Christmas.

Hey, where are
we going?

Oooh, it's
sparkly in here.
Are all those
presents
for ME?

Wait one stinkin', stompin' minute!

I'm on the Christmas tree? On the very TOP? This is . . . WOW! It's like . . . It's like I'm riding in Santa's sleigh! It's a Cookiesaurus Christmas!

Hey, Santa! Look at me— no hands!

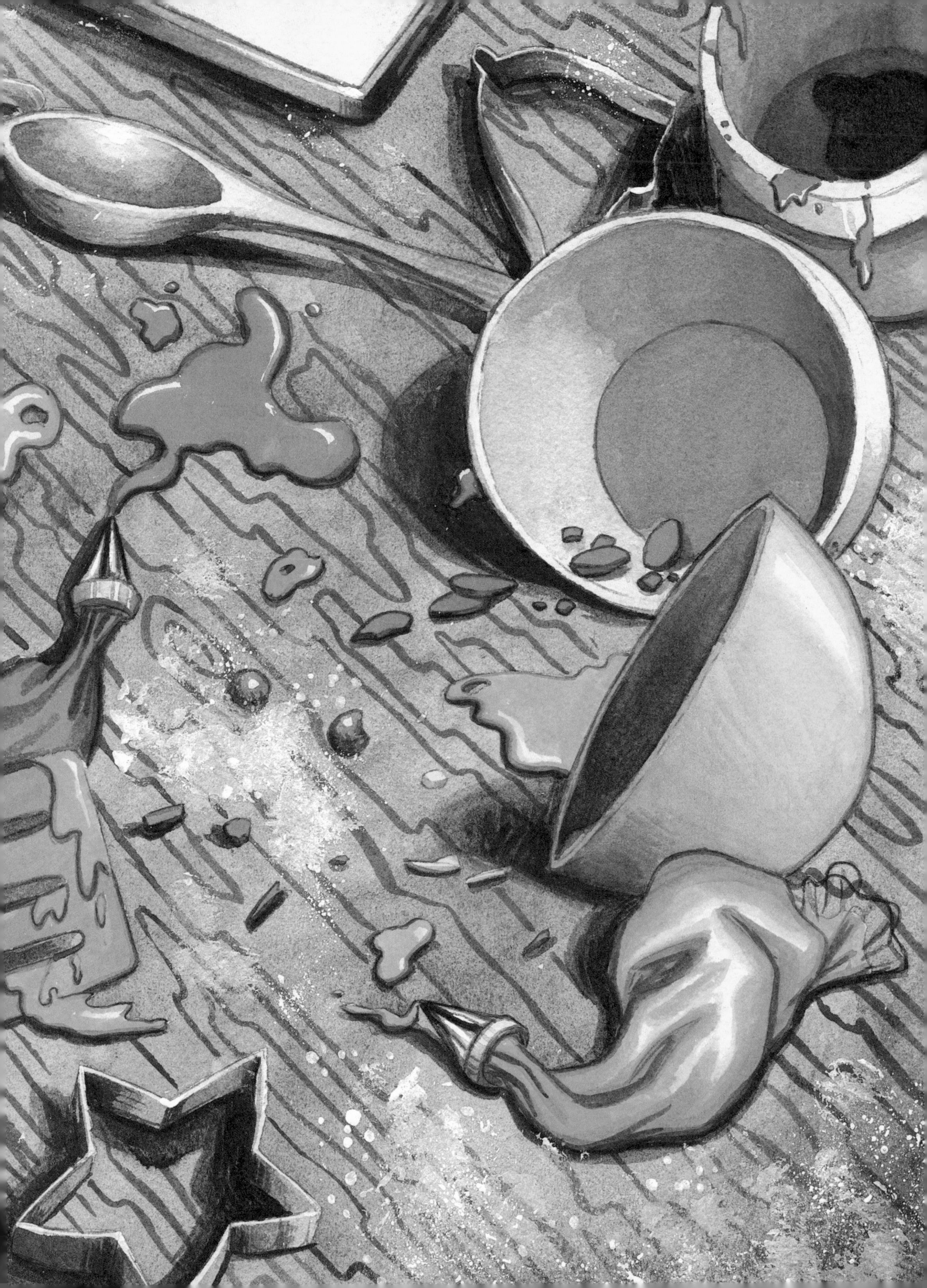

Amy Fellner Dominy previously collaborated with Nate Evans and AG Ford on *Cookiesaurus Rex*. She is also an author of teen and tween novels, including *Die for You*, *A Matter of Heart*, *Audition & Subtraction*, and *OyMG*, a Sydney Taylor Notable Book for Teens. Amy earned an MFA in playwriting, and her plays for adults and children have been staged across the country. Amy lives with her family in Phoenix, Arizona.

Nate Evans is the author or author-illustrator of more than forty children's books, including *Ponyella* with Laura Numeroff and *BANG! BOOM! ROAR! A Busy Crew of Dinosaurs*. Before turning to his true love—children's books—he was a greeting card artist. Nate is also a seventh-grade English teacher and loves to share his passion for books with his students. He lives in Gilbert, Arizona.

AG Ford is a *New York Times* best-selling illustrator and the recipient of two NAACP Image Awards. He has published more than fifteen children's books, with such authors as Kareem Abdul-Jabbar, Sharon Robinson, Ilyasah Shabazz, Martin Luther King III, Nick Cannon, Jonah Winter, and Archbishop Desmond Tutu. He lives in Frisco, Texas, with his wife, Brandy, and their son, Maddox.